Peanut Butter
& Jellyous

To friendship, in its many forms, thank you for the support,
inspiration, and love—*MG*

For my wife Erin. We go together like PB&J!—*SM*

Published by
MAGINATION PRESS ®
An Educational Publishing Foundation Book
American Psychological Association
750 First Street NE
Washington, DC 20002

Magination Press is a registered trademark of the American Psychological Association.

For more information about our books, including a complete catalog, please write to us,
call 1-800-374-2721, or visit our website at www.apa.org/pubs/magination.

Book design by Sandra Kimbell
Printed by Worzalla, Stevens Point, WI
Peach Fuzz font by Typadelic

Library of Congress Cataloging-in-Publication Data
Names: Genhart, Michael, author. | Mack, Steve (Steve Page), illustrator.
Title: Peanut Butter & jellyous : ...sometimes friendships
   get sticky / by Michael Genhart, PhD ;
   illustrated by Steve Mack.
Other titles: Peanut Butter and jellyous, sometimes
   friendships get sticky
Description: Washington, DC : Magination Press,
   [2017] | Summary: Peanut Butter and Jelly
   are very good friends, but when Peanut Butter
   tries to spend time with others, Jelly becomes
   very jealous until Peanut Butter helps her find
   new friends, too.
Identifiers: LCCN 2016049653| ISBN 9781433823374
   (hardcover) | ISBN 1433823373 (hardcover)
Subjects: | CYAC: Best friends—Fiction. |
   Friendship—Fiction. | Jealousy—Fiction. |
   Food—Fiction.
Classification: LCC PZ7.1.G47 Pe 2017 |
DDC [E]—dc23 LC record available at
https://lccn.loc.gov/2016049653

Manufactured in the United States of America
10 9 8 7 6 5 4 3 2 1

Peanut Butter
& Jellyous

...sometimes friendships get sticky

by Michael Genhart, PhD

illustrated by Steve Mack

Magination Press • Washington, DC
American Psychological Association

Most days I feel pretty smooth.

Sometimes I can be extra nutty.

And on tough days, I can be kind of crunchy.

But with my best friend, Jelly, well, we make quite a combo.

She is very sweet.

She adds color and flavor to whatever we do.

We stick together.

Peanut Butter and Jelly.
Jelly and Peanut Butter.

We are ALWAYS together.

But sometimes I like to hang out with others.

That makes Jelly very sad.

She even gets mad. She's afraid
she'll lose me as a friend if I'm
friends with someone else too.

Like the time I tried to be friends with—

Banana…and she went bananas!

and with Honey...she delivered quite a sting!

and then came Chocolate…she just got steaming hot!

Jelly tried really hard to get in
the way of these friendships.

One time, I got together with Celery and Raisins to play "Ants on a Log."

Jelly flipped her lid—and created a very sticky *log jam!*

Jelly got very jellyous!

I didn't know what to do.

It felt like I had to choose between Jelly and my new friends.
That's not a choice I wanted.

Then I had an idea.

Jelly could meet some new friends of her own—

so Jelly met Crumpet…that was triumphant!

and she met Toast...and they made a toast.

and then Tea joined in...and they had a party.

Jelly went from feeling very sad to getting really mad
to being glad she met new friends.

And when Jelly felt glad, I felt glad too.

It hasn't been easy, but now there's more room for other friends.

And, of course, always for each other.
PB & J. We'll always be a classic duo…

...now with even more friendships to share!

Note to Parents, Caregivers, and Educators

Peanut Butter & Jellyous is a playful story about dealing with jealous feelings in a friendship when two kids are best friends and new friends enter the mix. Jealousy can erupt in upset and anger, and become destructive to a friendship. The answer to jealousy in a friendship isn't always to include the new friends in the original friendship. Sometimes this outcome works, and when it does all parties can benefit. Another developmental step in the land of friendships is being able to maintain the original friendship while also forming significant bonds with others separately, as Jelly learns to do in this story. Whatever the outcome, coming up with suitable solutions and coping skills when facing jealous feelings is important. The good news is there are ways we as parents and educators can help the children in our lives with these complex and sometimes painful feelings.

What Is Jealousy?

Jealousy and envy are normal human emotions. And though the terms are often used interchangeably, they are not the same thing. Envy involves two people while jealousy involves a third person. With envy you feel that you are lacking something that someone else has, and you want that thing. A child may envy another's skills, abilities, or characteristics—for example, how fast a classmate can run. A child may also envy someone else's things or experiences—for example, another classmate's trip to Disneyworld or new bicycle.

With jealousy you feel a kind of threat that you could lose something or someone to another person. Your child might fear that their best friend likes another child better than

them, and fear being replaced. Jealousy also often emerges when a new baby arrives in the family, requiring lots of parental time; if an older sibling is getting attention for achievements or is allowed to do things like stay up longer at night; or when a parent, following a divorce, is dating others. In each case a young child can fear losing time, attention, and love. While *Peanut Butter & Jellyous* focuses on jealousy in the context of a friendship, some of the strategies in this Note may be useful for dealing with other types of jealousy and envy as well.

Signs of Jealousy

When a child is feeling jealousy, it may not always be obvious. It can sometimes be hidden in a child's behavior. For example, your child might complain of "tummy aches" or other physical symptoms, feel helpless and easily give up on things when normally this would not be the case, withdraw from a friendship, become less available to a friend, or begin to be less supportive of a friend particularly if that friend has experienced something positive. A child might start to be quite critical of a friend or even talk about that friend in ugly ways to other children. Alternatively, you might hear a child exaggerate happiness about a friendship or become very cautious, warning their friend to "be careful" of their new friend.

More obvious indicators of jealousy include overt anger and aggression expressed toward a friend or the "new" friend; bullying, teasing, or being mean to the target of jealousy; revenge-seeking or sabotaging behavior (e.g., telling lies about others to bring them down or about oneself just to be liked best); and clingy, possessive, and demanding overtures toward the best friend so as to not let that child wander off to other friends.

What You Can Do to Help

The following are some ways you can help your child learn to cope with their feelings of jealousy.

- **Make time to talk.** Listen to your child talk about their fears without taking over the conversation or rushing in to solve the problem. If your child fears losing a friend, feeling less than, or being left out, find out through active listening how your child is interpreting interactions with others. You might help your child with possible misinterpretations of a social situation. Role-play these social interactions with your child to help articulate their feelings and possible solutions. Drawing pictures or writing songs with your child about the problems they are encountering can also get to the heart of what they are feeling. Let your child know that it's okay to feel as they do, but that acting on these feelings in a negative way is not okay.

- **Show empathy.** Show that you understand your child's feelings. For example, you can say something like, "I see why you feel upset about not being included in Susan's party. She's new to your class and is spending a lot of time with your friend." As a parent or teacher, you can point out that as much as things feel "definite" ("We will never be friends again!" or "They seem like they are going to be best friends forever!" or "Every time I get a best friend I end up losing that friend!"), things can change and they often do so.

- **Teach gratitude.** Teaching gratitude, especially through modeling it as a parent, is showing your child the opposite of jealousy. Discuss family values where more emphasis is placed on what one already has, experiences, family time together, and important intangibles like feeling loved and supported. Together with your child, you can brainstorm a "Gratitude Checklist" of things they are thankful for. The checklist should include positive attributes like "how well swimming is going because of all the practice you are putting into it." A child who is experiencing jealousy may be focusing on what they do not have and feeling crummy about that. This exercise can interrupt and reduce those feelings.

- **Celebrate differences.** Notice with your child how everyone is different. Help your child see how much we learn from differences in people.

If your child envies someone else's qualities—for example, their curly red hair, or gymnastics ability—help your child to see how these different attributes and skills might complement your child's own strengths.

- **Read together.** Read and discuss stories about the challenges of jealous feelings. In addition to **Peanut Butter & Jellyous,** try some of these books: *When I Feel Jealous* by Cornelia Spelman; *What To Do When It's Not Fair: A Kid's Guide to Handling Envy and Jealousy* by Jacqueline B. Toner and Claire A. B. Freeland; *Me, Too!* by Annika Dunklee; and *Do You Still Love Me?* by Charlotte Middleton. These books can be read and re-read. Ask questions and start conversations with your child about the themes in the books. In these discussions, it can also be a good time to share your family values with your child. That is, while your son or daughter might be preoccupied with jealousy about having something, how high someone can jump, or how a friend is paying more attention to someone else, you might talk about what it means to show caring, forgiveness, and generosity toward others, or what it means to try hard at something even though there may be obstacles.

- **Give examples from your own life.** Talk with your child about times when you have felt jealous and what you learned from those experiences. You might illustrate through your story how these feelings come and go and how they can diminish if you let them. For example, your story could point out how "first" thoughts, when feeling jealous, can steer someone in a very wrong direction. Show that by being thoughtful first one can be less reactive in how one behaves later.

- **Model compassion.** If your child is on the receiving end of jealous feelings, check in with them if they are in any way contributing to the friend's jealousy. Some children are in a hurry to show off their own successes and don't realize that this behavior could trigger jealousy in someone else. Ask your child to consider whether their friend might be having a hard time or is in a tough spot. Acknowledge that this friend must be really hurting to have said ugly words. This show of empathy is very hard to do!

- **Manage stress.** General stress can also contribute to a child having difficulty thinking clearly about these matters. Consistent exercise, relaxation techniques, yoga, and plenty of time for play and fun are just some of the ways children can reduce the overall stress they carry around.

- **Make room for many different friendships.** Host inclusive events and activities with several friends together but also make time for best friends to continue to have their time together and strengthen these ties.

- **Encourage a positive self-image.** What are your child's positive skills, abilities, and characteristics? Periodically take stock of these with your child. Remind your son or daughter how they contribute to friendships in beneficial ways (e.g., by displays of kindness and support) and what they do that makes their friendships successful. And help them to remember to be proud of these successful friendships!

- **Help with deciding when a friendship is no longer friendly.** Over time if there is no improvement in the tension in a friendship, it may be time to consider ending it. Continuing to be in a friendship that has turned toxic and has not gotten better will have an adverse impact on both parties. Help your child to appreciate when it's time to no longer nurture a relationship that does not feel nurturing.

If your child continues to have problems with jealous feelings or dealing with a friend who is expressing jealousy, it might be time to seek professional guidance. Having a therapist to talk these matters out with can help. Play therapy or talk therapy (depending on the age of the child) can help elicit underlying feelings connected to jealousy.

About the Author

Michael Genhart, PhD, is a licensed clinical psychologist in private practice in San Francisco and Mill Valley, California. He lives with his family in Marin County. He received his BA in psychology from the University of California, San Diego and his PhD in clinical and community psychology from the University of Maryland, College Park. He is the author of several picture books including: *Ouch! Moments: When Words Are Used in Hurtful Ways* (2016), *So Many Smarts!* (2017), *Mac & Geeeez!* (2017), *Cake & I Scream!* (2017), and *I See You* (2017), all from Magination Press, as well as *Yes We Are!* (Little Pickle Press, 2018).

About the Illustrator

Steve Mack grew up a prairie boy on Canada's Great Plains and has drawn for as long as he can remember. His first lessons in art were taught to him by watching his grandfather do paint-by-numbers at the summer cottage. He has worked for greeting card companies and has illustrated several books. Steve lives in a beautiful valley in a turn-of-the-century farmhouse with his wife and two children.

About Magination Press

Magination Press is an imprint of the American Psychological Association, the largest scientific and professional organization representing psychologists in the United States and the largest association of psychologists worldwide.